THE PERFECT SALES PITCH: MYTH OR REALITY?

FROM PITCHING TO PARTNERING—THE VIKAS JAIN WAY

VIKAS KRISHNA KUMAR JAIN

Dedicated in loving memory of **my mother, Sapna Jain**, whose values and wisdom continue to guide every step I take.

My loving late mother, Sapna Jain

Contents

Dedication

To all the passionate sales professionals I've coached,
whose questions, stories, and relentless spirit inspired this book.
And to my family, whose unwavering support and patience
make every pitch—and every dream—possible.

— Vikas Jain

To my father, **Mr. Krishna Kumar Jain,** whose strength and unwavering support has been my greatest inspiration.

To my wonderful sisters, **Yojana Jain and Shilpy Jain,** who have always stood by me through life's ups and downs.

To my loving wife, **Rakhi Jain,** and my amazing son, **Ranbir Jain**—your love and encouragement fuel my dreams every day.

And finally, to my sweetest companion, **Bruno**—your unconditional affection and cheerful spirit make every day brighter.

This book exists because of all of you.

— Vikas Jain (Baba)

Vikas Jain

Vikas Krishna Kumar Jain

Preface

Over the past eighteen years, I've had the privilege of coaching hundreds of talented sales professionals. Throughout this journey, I've consistently observed one undeniable truth: sales isn't merely about products, features, or even persuasion—it's fundamentally about people, connection, and trust.

When I first began my career, I, like many others, struggled with the traditional methods of selling. I quickly learned that generic pitches and cookie-cutter approaches weren't just ineffective—they were counterproductive. In today's digital-first era, customers are more informed, skeptical, and discerning than ever before. They crave authenticity, value, and genuine understanding from the people hoping to sell to them.

In response to these evolving expectations, I started refining my own approach, developing methods that not only close deals but also forge meaningful, long-lasting relationships. This journey inspired what I now call "Precision Persona Strategy"—a core philosophy that emphasizes personalized messaging, storytelling, empathy, and meticulous preparation. It's the foundation of every sales pitch I've crafted since then, and it's a core concept throughout this book.

This book is not just a collection of theories. It's filled with practical insights, proven strategies, and real-world examples drawn directly from the experiences of myself and the incredible sales teams I've coached. My hope is that as you turn these pages, you'll find the clarity, confidence, and tools you need to master your own sales conversations.

Whether you're a seasoned professional looking to sharpen your skills, or someone at the start of your sales career seeking guidance, this book is designed to help you move beyond transactional pitches and toward building genuine, trust-based connections.

Sales, at its very best, is about adding value to the lives of others. With each chapter, you'll discover how to craft sales pitches that resonate deeply, convert effectively, and leave a lasting positive impact on every client you meet.

Welcome to the journey of turning your pitch into your greatest strength.

Warm regards,

Vikas Jain

Sales Coach, Consultant & Author

Prologue

It was a crisp winter morning in January when I walked into what felt like the most important meeting of my career. I had spent weeks preparing for this pitch—meticulously researching the client, rehearsing every word, and creating a presentation I believed was flawless. Yet, within the first few minutes, I realized I had already lost the room.

The executives seated across from me had clearly done their homework too, and my neatly scripted pitch—full of generic statistics, familiar benefits, and standard corporate jargon—was falling flat. They'd heard it all before. In that moment, my heart sank. I knew my service could help them immensely, yet my message wasn't resonating.

As I left that office empty-handed, a thought kept echoing through my mind: "What went wrong?"

It took a while, but the answer eventually became crystal clear: the perfect sales pitch isn't about having the best slides, the slickest presentation, or even the strongest features. It's about understanding people deeply, connecting with their reality, and earning their trust.

That pivotal meeting marked the start of my journey into a new era of selling—one built not on memorized scripts but on genuine empathy, meticulous personalization, and powerful storytelling. Since then, I've had countless opportunities to test, refine, and teach this approach. The results have transformed not only my career but also the careers of the many sales professionals I've had the honor to coach.

This book is the culmination of that journey. It's a practical guide, born from real-world successes and failures, designed to help you bypass the costly mistakes I once made. Inside these pages, you'll find proven frameworks, actionable strategies, and personal anecdotes that demonstrate exactly how to craft sales pitches that resonate, persuade, and close deals—not just occasionally, but consistently.

If you've ever wondered whether the perfect sales pitch is real or merely a myth, you're in the right place. Join me as we explore this powerful question together, diving deep into the heart of sales excellence, human connection, and trust.

Let's begin.

Vikas Jain

Sales Coach, Consultant & Author

ONE

THE NEW ERA OF SALES

? Why Traditional Sales Pitches No Longer Work

Once upon a time, a sales pitch was the make-or-break moment. A salesperson would walk into a room, flip open a laptop, run through a presentation, and—if all went well—walk out with a handshake and a deal. It was a process built on scripts, feature lists, and flashy presentations. And for years, it worked.

But not anymore.

Today, that same pitch—no matter how polished—is often met with glazed eyes, polite nods, or worse, a complete lack of follow-up. The problem isn't just that salespeople are using outdated tactics. The problem is that buyers have changed, and sales pitches haven't.

We're living in the age of informed decision-making. Buyers don't wait for a salesperson to educate them—they've already done the homework. They've read product reviews, visited your competitors' websites, checked your founders on LinkedIn, compared pricing models, and maybe even tested free trials.

They don't need more information. They need insight, clarity, and confidence.

Unfortunately, many pitches are still built to inform, not connect. They're loaded with features instead of relevance, loaded with slides instead of stories, and they speak more about the seller than about the buyer.

That's why traditional sales pitches no longer work. The rules of the game have changed. And if you want to win, your approach must evolve too.

? *How Buyer Behavior Has Fundamentally Changed*

Let's pause and reflect on this simple question:

When was the last time you made a significant purchase without researching it first?

Just like you, today's buyers come armed with context, comparisons, and questions. They don't want to be "pitched to"—they want to be understood. They want to know:

Do you get my pain points?

Have you solved this for someone like me before?

Can I trust you to deliver what you promise?

This shift in buyer behavior isn't just a trend—it's a transformation.

In B2B sales, the average buyer now engages with 5 to 7 pieces of content before speaking to a sales rep. Over 70% of their buying journey happens online, and by the time they do talk to someone, they've already built expectations around what they need and who might deliver it best.

What does this mean for you?

It means that your pitch needs to do more than inform—it needs to align with what they already know and add something they didn't expect: a new perspective, a valuable insight, a tailored solution, or a powerful story that changes how they see their problem.

Buyers today don't want to be convinced—they want to be understood and empowered. Your pitch must become the bridge between what they think they need and what they didn't even know was possible.

?⚲♂? *Why This Book—and Why Vikas Jain?*

I wrote this book because I've lived this shift.

Over the past 18 years, I've founded and scaled three companies—Marastu (a performance-driven digital marketing agency), Comfroi (an eCommerce growth firm with a pay-on-results model), and Perfozi (a platform that trains and places performance-ready sales professionals). Across these ventures, I've sat in hundreds of high-stakes meetings, crafted thousands of pitches, and coached sales teams across industries, geographies, and markets.

But what I'm most proud of isn't just the deals closed. It's the evolution I've seen in the people I've worked with—the confidence they build when they stop memorizing scripts and start speaking with relevance, empathy, and clarity.

That transformation is what this book is about.

This isn't a book of clichés or generic advice. It's a practical guide grounded in real experiences—the successes, the stumbles, and the breakthroughs that come from being in the trenches of modern selling.

You'll find frameworks like the Precision Persona Strategy (PPS) that I developed and teach to help sellers understand buyer psychology. You'll see real-life pitch examples that worked—and why. And you'll walk away with actionable tactics to apply in your very next conversation.

Whether you're a founder, a solo consultant, a corporate sales rep, or a team leader, this book will help you craft pitches that don't just sound good—they work.

Because the truth is:

The perfect sales pitch isn't a myth. It's just misunderstood.

Let's change that—together.

Rethinking the Sales Pitch in the Age of Informed Buyers

Let me conclude this chapter with a harsh but liberating truth:

Most sales pitches fail—not because the product isn't good, but because the pitch isn't relevant.

Gone are the days when prospects needed a salesperson to tell them what a product does. In the age of Google, LinkedIn, YouTube demos, and customer reviews, buyers walk into conversations with 70–80% of their decision already made. They've read your case studies. They've compared your pricing. They've even peeked at your founders' LinkedIn profiles.

So, what are they looking for in a conversation with you?

They're looking for clarity. For confidence. For someone who understands their world better than a search engine ever could.

? The Pitch Isn't the Problem—It's the Approach

When I launched Marastu, our early goal was to become a performance-driven digital marketing agency. We had a strong team, good results, and impressive case studies. But our close rate during the first quarter was less than 10%. Surprising, right?

That's when I sat down and reviewed every sales call, every email, and every proposal we had sent out. What I discovered changed everything: our pitch was focused on us—our capabilities, our portfolio, our tools.

It wasn't until we flipped the script and started centering our pitch entirely on the client's business, their pain points, and their buyer journey that things turned around. We stopped pitching services and started diagnosing problems.

The result? In the very next quarter, our close rate jumped to 28%. By the end of the year, we had doubled our revenue—and none of that came from increasing our ad spend or hiring more salespeople. It came from refining our pitch.

? *Real-World Example #1: From Rejected to Retained – A Marastu Turnaround*

One of our earlier prospects at Marastu—a SaaS company based in the UK—initially declined our proposal. Their feedback? "You sound just like the other five agencies we spoke to."

Instead of writing them off, I replied with a simple message:

"Would you be open to a 10-minute conversation—not to sell, but to help you break down where the real performance gaps might be in your current strategy?"

They agreed. In that call, I used what I now call the Precision Persona Strategy (PPS)—a framework I developed to align sales messaging with specific buyer personas. We showed them not what we did, but how they were losing opportunities in their funnel due to misaligned messaging across platforms. The entire conversation was about them, not us.

They signed a 6-month contract the next week. Today, they're one of our longest-standing clients.

? Trust Is the New Currency

Fast-forward to when we launched **Comfroi**, a brand built specifically to serve eCommerce businesses. Unlike traditional agencies, Comfroi doesn't just build and market stores—we partner with clients on a Performance Partnership Model (PPM). That means: we only make money when they do.

Now, imagine pitching that to a skeptical store owner who's been burned by three agencies in the past.

Our first few pitches fell flat. Why? Because we were focusing on the model—PPM—without showing them what it meant in their reality.

We reframed our approach. Instead of saying, "We work on a performance model," we began saying things like:

"We take full accountability. If your store doesn't grow, neither do we. Let me show you how a brand like yours scaled their Shopify revenue from $5K/month to $40K/month in six months—with zero upfront investment."

By using storytelling and relatable results, we moved from a conceptual pitch to a visual and emotional one. That's when our pipeline opened up.

Today, Comfroi's pitch deck starts with a single line:

"We don't offer services. We offer results—and we only get paid when you win."

And believe me, that hits harder than any award badge on a homepage.

? *Real-World Example #2: How Perfozi Closes Without "Selling"*

With Perfozi, my mission was to address a long-standing issue in the hiring industry—misaligned expectations between businesses and sales hires. We built a model where companies hire trained professionals and get weekly performance coaching from me personally.

But how do you pitch "sales coaching for your sales hire" without sounding like an added cost?

Here's the pitch I used with one of our first clients:

"You don't just want a salesperson. You want results. What if I told you we place professionals and ensure their performance week after week through guided strategies and personal coaching, so you're not left babysitting your own sales team?"

That single sentence led to a trial. Two months in, the founder told me:

"I've never felt so confident handing over lead conversion to someone I didn't hire myself."

The lesson? Your pitch shouldn't sell the service. It should sell the solution to their fear.

? The Shift You Need to Make Today

The best sales pitch is no longer about delivering a "wow" moment.

It's about:

Making your prospect feel understood

Framing their pain in ways they haven't articulated themselves

Offering a path to clarity and control

Earning trust—not just attention

As we explore the rest of this book, you'll learn how to build pitches that do exactly that. You'll uncover frameworks, questions, and formats that work not just in theory—but in the real world.

Because here's the truth I've learned over and over again:

A perfect pitch doesn't exist in a template. It exists in your understanding of the person you're speaking to.

Welcome to the new world of selling. :)

TWO
Understanding the Modern Sales Pitch

? What Exactly Is a Sales Pitch?

A sales pitch is often misunderstood. For many, it brings to mind a rehearsed speech, a flashy PowerPoint, or a cold call that gets ignored within seconds. But in today's buyer-driven world, a sales pitch is something much more nuanced, and much more human.

A sales pitch is a strategic conversation that connects your solution to your prospect's need—clearly, quickly, and credibly.

Whether you're sending a two-minute video message, jumping on a discovery Zoom call, or presenting to a stakeholder panel, your pitch is your moment to answer one key question:

"Can you solve my problem better than anyone else?"

If your answer isn't immediately clear, personalized, and persuasive, the opportunity slips away.

? *The Psychology Behind Persuasion*

In every sales interaction, you're not just speaking to a business—you're speaking to a person. A person with priorities, doubts, deadlines, KPIs, and yes, fears.

Most decisions—yes, even in B2B—are made emotionally first, and then justified logically. That's why a pitch that hits only the head often misses the heart. The most effective salespeople speak to both.

As a seller, your pitch must activate:

- **Relevance — "This is built for me."**
- **Confidence — "You clearly know what you're doing."**
- **Urgency — "We need to act on this now."**

Let me show you how this played out in real conversations I've had with clients across the globe.

? *Real-World Example: Marastu's Video Call with a SaaS Company in the UK*

In mid-2023, I (Vikas Jain) was on a video call with a growth-stage SaaS company based in Manchester. The CMO and Head of Demand Gen were present, and they were actively considering a new agency to lead their paid campaigns.

They had already spoken to two UK-based agencies before us, and I could sense they were drained from hearing the same old promises—"We'll optimize your ROAS," "We specialize in B2B," "We use AI tools."

Instead of presenting my slide deck, I said:

"I'd love to understand what hasn't worked with the last agency. What made you start looking again?"

That question flipped the dynamic instantly.

They opened up. The issue wasn't clicks or impressions—it was inconsistent lead quality and a disconnect between ad messaging and sales conversion.

That changed everything.

I ditched the prepared deck and shared a real-time Notion board showing how we helped a similar US-based SaaS company increase qualified leads by 63%—not just traffic. We walked through landing page copies, lead scoring techniques, and how sales enablement needs to match ad intent.

By the end of that call, the CMO said:

"This is the first time an agency has actually talked about our funnel rather than their services."

We signed a 6-month pilot the following week. That's the power of understanding the psychology behind what the buyer truly needs.

? From Interruption to Interaction

Traditional pitches are often built to interrupt:

"Let me tell you what we do." "Here's our story." "We've worked with 50+ clients."

But the modern pitch needs to involve.

Let's look at how this came to life during a stakeholder call for Comfroi—my eCommerce-focused performance agency—with a client from Australia.

? Real-World Example: Comfroi's Interactive Pitch to an Australian Apparel Brand

We were pitching our Performance Partnership Model (PPM) to a Melbourne-based D2C apparel brand. The founder, head of eCommerce, and digital marketing manager joined the Zoom call.

They had previously worked with three different Indian agencies that charged monthly retainers without delivering significant growth.

Instead of showing a "why we're better" deck, I said:

"Can we open your Shopify analytics together and map out your revenue patterns?"

That unexpected question grabbed their attention.

We pulled up their data, noted gaps in returning customer revenue, weak email automation flows, and inconsistent product margins.

Then I said:

"What if we create a growth plan together—with realistic targets—and we only get paid when you hit them?"

By co-creating their growth roadmap in real time, we turned a one-way pitch into a two-way strategy session.

They signed us within 72 hours. Why? Because we didn't sell services—we shared ownership.

? How Vikas Jain Redefined the Sales Approach

Over the years, my biggest realization as a founder and coach has been this:

"The perfect pitch isn't about delivering a message. It's about designing a moment—where the buyer feels seen, heard, and understood."

This realization led to the creation of my signature Precision Persona Strategy (PPS)—a model that helps salespeople identify the real buyer, their pain, and the emotional motivator behind their decisions.

One of the best examples of this came from a Perfozi video call with a San Francisco-based startup.

? Real-World Example: The Sales Hiring Pitch That Hit Home (Perfozi, USA)

A VC-backed US tech startup had just raised Series A and was hiring aggressively—but was struggling to find salespeople who could perform.

I joined the Zoom call with their COO and Head of Talent.

They were skeptical about hiring remotely from India.

I didn't start with CVs or pricing.

Instead, I opened with:

"Can I ask—what does a win look like for your sales team, three months from now? And what's keeping you up at night about it?"

They said, "We're tired of wasting time on onboarding. We need people who can start showing traction now."

That led to a conversation about how Perfozi candidates don't just come trained—they come with a custom scorecard, weekly accountability coaching, and 30-day ramp plans built with the founder's input.

I shared a Notion page live with our onboarding blueprint. They invited us to submit three profiles by the end of the week. Two were hired.

That pitch didn't land because of what I said—it worked because of how deeply we listened and how confidently we addressed fear.

? Key Takeaways from This Chapter

? A sales pitch is not a monologue—it's a diagnostic conversation.

? Focus on the buyer's emotions, not just logic.

? Ask meaningful, unscripted questions to shift from selling to co-solving.

? Use real-time tools (like dashboards, analytics, or documents) to make your pitch interactive.

? Build trust not by talking about yourself—but by talking about them in a way no one else has.

In the next chapter, we'll explore the Anatomy of a High-Impact Pitch—the structural elements that make a sales conversation powerful, persuasive, and memorable. We'll break down how to create your pitch hook, frame pain points, deliver a strong value proposition, and end with a call to action that gets results.

Get ready to build your pitch—brick by brick.

— Vikas Jain

THREE

THE ANATOMY OF A HIGH-IMPACT PITCH

If selling today is about connection, not coercion—then your sales pitch needs a structure that doesn't feel like a pitch at all. It needs to feel like a natural conversation that gently guides the buyer toward realizing that your solution is exactly what they need.

Let's dive into the six essential components every high-impact sales pitch must have—supported by buyer psychology and real-world examples from my journey with Marastu, Comfroi, and Perfozi.

1. ? The Hook: Grabbing Attention Instantly

Psychological Principle:

Humans have short attention spans (8 seconds on average). The Reciprocity Bias says people pay attention to those who offer value first.

Your hook should create immediate value—either by showing you understand their problem, offering a surprising insight, or asking a provocative question.

Real-World Example:

? Marastu Video Call with a SaaS Client (London, UK)

Instead of opening with our agency intro, I said:

"Most SaaS companies I work with lose 35% of paid ad budgets because the sales messaging doesn't match landing page intent. I noticed a few gaps on your site too. May I show you?"

Result: Immediate engagement. Curiosity triggered.

They wanted to hear more.

Lesson:

Don't introduce yourself. Introduce a problem they didn't know they had.

2. ? The Problem: Articulating the Buyer's Pain Better Than They Can

Psychological Principle:

The Principle of Empathy states that when someone feels truly understood, they trust faster.

Your pitch should name their pain points with such clarity that the buyer says internally:

"Exactly! That's my problem."

Real-World Example:

? Comfroi Video Call with an Australian D2C Fashion Brand

Instead of asking, "What are your goals?", I said:

"Growing D2C brands often face two silent killers: rising ad costs and stagnating repeat customer rates. Looking at your Shopify numbers, I suspect retention is a bigger problem for you than acquisition. Does that sound right?"

Result:

The founder said:

"That's scarily accurate. No one pointed that out."

Lesson:

State their unspoken fears better than they can.
That's when they realize you understand them deeply.

3. ? The Value Proposition: Offering Transformation, Not Features

Psychological Principle:

The Vision Bias says people are more likely to act when they vividly imagine a better future.

Your pitch must paint a before-and-after picture:

Where they are now ▸ Where they could be with your solution.

Real-World Example:

? Marastu Campaign Pitch to a US Tech Company (San Diego)

Instead of saying, "We improve your paid ads," I said:

"Imagine if every $1 you spent on ads returned $6 in pipeline—not 3. Imagine if your sales team started their day calling warm leads instead of cold ones. That's the transformation we create."

Result:

Their CMO leaned in and said:

"Tell me how."

Lesson:

People don't buy services. They buy a better version of their future.

4. ? The Solution: Showing How Without Overloading Them

Psychological Principle:

Cognitive Load Theory teaches us that too much information overwhelms the brain.

Explain your solution simply. Make it feel easy, inevitable, and achievable.

Real-World Example:

? Comfroi Pitch to an Australian Skincare Brand (Sydney)

Instead of explaining complex funnel optimization, I said:

"We insert two growth levers: (1) Ads that speak to emotional needs at the top, and (2) Automated flows that nurture hesitant buyers at the bottom. It's like widening the river upstream and deepening it downstream."

Result:

The eCommerce manager said:

"Finally, someone who speaks human, not agency."

Lesson:

Keep your "how" simple. Complexity creates doubt. Simplicity builds belief.

5. ? Social Proof: Reducing Perceived Risk

Psychological Principle:

The Social Proof Bias shows that people fear being wrong alone but feel safer following others' choices.

Showing relatable success stories immediately lowers perceived risk.

Real-World Example:

? Perfozi Pitch to an Ahmedabad-Based IT Company

We were pitching a trained sales candidate to a SaaS firm in Ahmedabad.

Instead of just talking about skills, I said:

"Last month, a similar Ahmedabad-based IT firm onboarded a Perfozi-trained SDR. Within 45 days, he closed deals worth   ₹12 lakh. I can share their testimonial if you'd like."

Result:

The CEO replied:

"If someone like us saw results, we should at least try."

Lesson:

When in doubt, buyers lean on the experience of others.

6. ? Call to Action (CTA): Making the Next Step Frictionless

Psychological Principle:

Commitment & Consistency Principle shows that people are more likely to continue once they take a small initial step.

Never end your pitch vaguely ("Let me know"). Instead, suggest the next step clearly and easily.

Real-World Example:

? Perfozi Video Call with an Ahmedabad Startup

After explaining the value, instead of saying, "So what do you think?", I said:

"If you like, we can set up a quick 20-minute follow-up with two shortlisted candidates tomorrow. No commitment—just an introduction call. Shall I block your preferred time?"

Result:

They agreed instantly because the step felt easy and non-threatening.

Lesson:

Always end with a specific, easy, low-risk action.

? Summary of High-Impact Pitch Structure:

Stage	Purpose	Psychological Trigger
Hook	Grab instant attention	Curiosity, Reciprocity
Problem	Build empathy and trust	Empathy Principle
Value Prop	Paint a desirable future	Vision Bias
Solution	Show the path simply	Cognitive Load Theory
Social Proof	Remove doubt through evidence	Social Proof Bias
CTA	Secure a small commitment	Commitment Principle

Summary of High-Impact Pitch Structure:

Final Thought:

"An effective sales pitch doesn't feel like a pitch—it feels like a rescue."
The buyer should leave your conversation feeling relieved, hopeful, and excited—not sold to.

In the next chapter, we'll move deeper into how to prepare for the pitch itself—the research, personalization, and mindset needed before you even open your mouth.

Because a great pitch starts long before the meeting begins.

Let's dive into preparation next!

— Vikas Jain

FOUR
PREPARING FOR THE PERFECT PITCH

Research, Personalization, and Pre-Pitch Psychology

Most people think the pitch starts when you begin talking.
That's a myth.

The best sales pitches are won long before the first word is spoken.

In my experience—especially while working with international clients at Marastu, Comfroi, and Perfozi—the biggest differentiator between a good pitch and a winning one has always been this: preparation.

Whether you're speaking to a startup founder in New York, a retail brand in Sydney, or an HR manager in Ahmedabad, your success depends on how well you understand them before the pitch begins.

Let's break down exactly what goes into preparing for a perfect pitch—and how you can systemize this process without overthinking it.

? Why Preparation Matters More Than Ever

Psychological Insight:

The Halo Effect suggests that the first impression someone has of you colors everything you say afterward.

When you walk into a conversation already knowing about their company, their goals, their struggles—they immediately place you in the "trusted expert" category.

This shifts the power dynamic.

You're no longer selling.

You're advising.

? Step 1: Research the Person, Not Just the Company

The common mistake:

Most salespeople study the company—its website, its services, maybe its latest blog post.

The pro move:

Research the person you're pitching to. What are they posting about on LinkedIn? What past roles have they held? What do they care about?

? Real-World Example: Marastu's Close Call in New York

A few months ago, we were pitching a performance marketing retainer to a mid-size SaaS company in New York. The founder was known for being no-nonsense and data-driven—his LinkedIn posts were all about "marketing ROI," "waste in paid media," and "why agencies fail."

Before the call, I went deep:

- **Read his LinkedIn activity from the last 90 days**
- **Saw his podcast interview where he mentioned, "Most agencies can't connect ads to actual MRR"**
- **Noticed he was ex-HubSpot and liked visual dashboards**

So I built our pitch deck backward.

We didn't lead with services—we led with a mock performance dashboard that visualized how we would connect ad spend to pipeline and revenue. It included:

A sample MRR forecast

Real examples from our current clients

A simple, 3-step growth model

He joined the Zoom call, arms crossed. By the second slide, he said:
"Okay, I'm listening. This is different."
We closed the deal in 6 days.
Lesson: Research makes the buyer feel like the pitch is built for them, not just used on them.

? Step 2: Personalize the Pain Point

Psychological Insight:
The Confirmation Bias means people are more likely to believe something if it confirms what they already suspect.
Use this to your advantage:
Instead of asking, "What's your pain point?", say:
"Based on [research], I imagine [X problem] might be costing you time or revenue. Does that resonate?"
You're not guessing. You're diagnosing.

Real-World Example: Comfroi Pitch to a Fashion Brand in Melbourne

Before our pitch, we:

- **Checked their Facebook ad library**
- **Noted inconsistent creative messaging**
- **Found Trustpilot reviews showing customer retention complaints**

On the pitch call, I said:
"It seems like your brand storytelling is strong, but the messaging between your Facebook ads and product pages doesn't align. That might be hurting conversion and repeat sales."
The founder looked surprised and said:
"That's exactly what our team argued last week. You're the first agency to mention that."
Boom. Instant trust.

? Step 3: Study Their Market, Not Just Their Business

Most buyers don't live in a vacuum. They constantly compare themselves to competitors. If you can show that you know their market, you gain massive credibility.

Use tools like:

- **Google Trends**
- **SimilarWeb or BuiltWith**
- **Public review sites**
- **ProductHunt (for SaaS)**
- **Shopify app rankings (for D2C)**

Real-World Example: Perfozi Pitch to an Ahmedabad-Based IT Company

This company was struggling to find an SDR who could "sell globally."
Before the call, we:

- **Studied 3 similar IT firms from Ahmedabad who hired remote SDRs**
- **Compared their LinkedIn content and hiring style**
- **Built a mini SWOT matrix**

On the call, I said:
"While many IT companies in Ahmedabad hire based on cost, those who see results invest in coaching support after hiring. That's exactly what Perfozi delivers—recruits plus performance accountability."
Result:
The CEO said:
"You clearly understand the local context—and that makes a difference."
They onboarded two SDRs that month.

? Step 4: Prepare a Customized CTA

The worst way to end a pitch?
"Let me know your thoughts."
The best way?
"Can I send over a 3-point proposal tailored to the gaps we discussed—and we can take 15 minutes tomorrow to review it together?"

Make the next step feel easy, specific, and low risk.

Bonus tip:

Write two possible follow-up subject lines in advance. If they ghost you, use those as your nudge.

? Bonus: Create a Pitch Prep Checklist

Here's a framework I personally use before every high-stakes pitch:

? *Vikas Jain's 5-Minute Pre-Pitch Checklist*

Task	Why It Matters
☑ Research buyer on LinkedIn	Build rapport & relevance
☑ Read last 3 company posts	Show you're up to date
☑ Identify 1 likely pain point	Lead with insight
☑ Review 1 competitor	Add market awareness
☑ Prepare a specific CTA	End strong

Vikas Jain's 5-Minute Pre-Pitch Checklist

Final Words:

"A pitch is only as good as the research behind it."

When you show up knowing the buyer's context better than they expected, you're no longer just another vendor. You become an asset. A partner. A trusted advisor.

And trust me: people don't ghost trusted advisors. They invite them back.

In the next chapter, we'll explore how to use storytelling as your secret sales weapon—so your pitch isn't just informative, but unforgettable.

Because data converts minds, but stories capture hearts.

— Vikas Jain

FIVE

THE POWER OF STORYTELLING IN SALES

"Stories are remembered up to 22 times more than facts alone."
— Dr. Jennifer Aaker, Stanford Graduate School of Business

- **Data convinces.**
- **But stories?**
- **They stick.**
- **They move.**

They transform a sales pitch into a conversation people care about.

As a sales coach, agency founder, and pitch strategist, I've seen one consistent truth:

The salespeople who win deals aren't just great talkers—they're great storytellers.

And in this chapter, I'll show you exactly how to turn your pitch into a story that connects emotionally, engages intellectually, and persuades powerfully.

? Why Storytelling Works (According to Science)

Here's why storytelling isn't fluff—it's neuroscience.

When you tell a story:

- **It activates the sensory cortex, making people feel like they're experiencing the moment.**
- **It releases oxytocin, the "trust hormone," increasing connection.**
- **It lights up the emotional and rational centers of the brain simultaneously, helping your message land both logically and emotionally.**

Compare that to a list of bullet points or a standard feature rundown—and there's no competition.

? Storytelling in Sales: The Framework

Every winning sales story—whether in a 30-second cold call or a 20-slide presentation—follows this simple structure:

- The 3-Part Story Arc:
- The Struggle – What was going wrong?
- The Shift – What action or insight changed the game?
- The Success – What was the transformation and impact?

Let's explore each part through real-world examples from my work.

? Example 1: The Comfroi Story Told to a UK-Based Agency

? Client: A Shopify partner agency in Birmingham, UK
The Struggle
"They were losing clients because they couldn't manage performance campaigns in-house. Their customers wanted real results, but they only offered design/dev."
The Shift
"We partnered to become their white-label performance marketing wing. We ran ads for their clients under their brand, and they only paid us when results came in."
The Success

"In 4 months, they retained 3 at-risk clients, grew monthly revenue by £18K, and positioned themselves as a full-service Shopify expert."

? This story made them say:

"That's exactly what we're going through. Can you do this for us too?"

Lesson: A good story should make the buyer see themselves in it.

? *Example 2: Perfozi Story for an Ahmedabad SaaS Company*

? Client: A local Ahmedabad-based IT firm hiring remote SDRs for the first time

The Struggle

"They had hired 3 salespeople in the past year. All underperformed. No process. No structure. Just chaos."

The Shift

"They approached Perfozi. We not only placed a trained SDR—we set up a weekly coaching rhythm, tracked KPIs, and aligned their CRM with a clear sales pipeline."

The Success

"In 45 days, their SDR closed two inbound deals and set up 17 qualified meetings. For the first time, the founder said, 'I'm not chasing reports anymore—I'm seeing momentum.'"

? The buyer on the video call said:

"This doesn't sound like hiring. This sounds like peace of mind."

Lesson: Every founder doesn't just want results—they want relief.

? *Example 3: Marastu Pitch to a US-based Fintech Company*

? Client: A startup in Miami, Florida running lead-gen ads for B2B lending

The Struggle

"They were pouring $20K/month into Google Ads, but their conversion rate was stuck at 0.6%. Their CAC was over $300."

The Shift

"Our team audited their funnel and realized the disconnect: their ad promised 'flexible funding in 48 hours,' but the landing page had 7 fields and a delayed response. We aligned the copy, streamlined the form, and automated pre-qualification emails."

The Success

"Conversion jumped to 2.1%. CAC dropped to $112. In 60 days, they 2.5x'd their deal flow—and paused ads because their sales team couldn't handle the volume."

? What closed the deal?

Not the numbers. Not the deck. But the story.

Lesson: A story that resolves a common frustration does more than convince—it reassures.

? *Types of Stories You Should Prepare*

Here are 4 types of stories every salesperson or founder should keep in their toolkit:

Type	Purpose
Customer Success Story	Shows real-world results buyers can relate to
Founder Origin Story	Builds credibility and emotional connection
Failure-to-Win Story	Demonstrates honesty, resilience, and growth
Vision Story	Inspires belief in your future partnership together

Types of Stories You Should Prepare

? *How to Integrate Stories into Your Pitch*

Here's how I personally coach teams to insert storytelling without it feeling scripted:

Start your pitch with a "frustration opener"

"Most of our clients come to us after trying 2-3 agencies and getting nothing but clicks and chaos."

Embed stories into problem-solution transitions

"Let me show you how we solved a similar issue for another client."

Use mini-stories in objection handling

"That's exactly what another founder told me—until we ran their first 7-day campaign."

Close with a vision story

"If this works like I expect, here's what your business could look like in 90 days..."

? Psychological Triggers Inside Every Good Story

Here's what storytelling activates in the brain—and why it matters in sales:

Trigger	What it Does
Empathy	Builds trust and emotional connection
Familiarity	Reduces fear by showing real examples
Social Proof	Reinforces credibility
Mirror Neurons	Makes the buyer *feel* like they're experiencing it
Contrast	Highlights change (from struggle to success)

Psychological Triggers Inside Every Good Story

? Final Thought

"Your customer won't remember your slide titles.
They'll remember the story you told that made them feel understood."

In a world of automation and overused sales scripts, storytelling is your most human advantage.

So, if you want your pitch to close deals, don't just pitch features—share moments.

Don't just talk data—deliver transformation through narrative.

Because when logic says maybe, a good story says yes.

Coming Up Next:

In Chapter 6, we'll talk about Personalization at Scale—how to tailor your pitch for different personas and roles (CEO, CMO, HR head, etc.) without rebuilding your deck every time.

Let's unlock how to make every prospect feel like the pitch was made just for them.

— Vikas Jain

SIX

PERSONALIZING YOUR PITCH FOR EVERY BUYER PERSONA

"People don't want to feel sold to—they want to feel understood."
— Vikas Jain

In sales, one of the most costly mistakes is treating every prospect the same.

You might have the right product, the right case study, even the right timing—but if you deliver a generic pitch, you risk sounding like everyone else.

This chapter is about precision—understanding who you're speaking to and tailoring your message so specifically that the buyer feels like the pitch was built just for them.

? Why Personalization Works (Psychology of Relevance)

Psychological Insight:

The Reticular Activating System (RAS) in the brain filters information and only lets in what it deems relevant or important.

- **When a buyer hears a pitch that:**
- **Uses their industry language**

- **Addresses their unique role**
- **Solves their problem**

Their RAS lights up—and they start paying full attention.

Personalization isn't a bonus—it's a requirement in today's high-stakes, low-patience market.

? The 3 Layers of Personalization

- **Role-Based – Tailor your pitch to their job function (e.g., CMO vs. CTO)**
- **Industry-Based – Speak the language of their vertical (e.g., D2C vs. SaaS)**
- **Company/Stage-Based – Align with their current maturity level (startup vs. enterprise)**

Let's walk through each with examples from my work at Marastu, Comfroi, and Perfozi.

?|? 1. Role-Based Personalization: Who Are You Speaking To?

Persona	What They Care About	How to Adjust Your Pitch
Founder/CEO	Growth, profitability, investor confidence	Focus on ROI, competitive edge, and time saved
CMO	Leads, brand, funnel performance	Focus on marketing KPIs, messaging alignment
Sales Head	Conversion rates, pipeline, CRM quality	Focus on qualified leads, sales velocity
HR Head	Talent performance, retention	Focus on onboarding ease, accountability
CTO/IT	Tech stack, data integrity, security	Talk integrations, load speed, scalability

Role-Based Personalization

? Example: Marastu Pitch to a CMO in the US vs. a Founder

? Client: B2B SaaS company in Chicago

To the CMO, we said:

"Let's reduce your CPL by 30% by aligning ad copy with what Sales is actually saying on calls. That will lower bounce and boost funnel quality."

To the Founder, we said:

"Your CAC is currently $280. We can bring it down to $150, while maintaining deal velocity. That impacts your bottom line directly."

? Same solution—different lens.

This created instant relevance for each stakeholder.

? 2. Industry-Based Personalization

Every industry has its own language, challenges, and metrics.

Your pitch must reflect those nuances to build credibility fast.

Industry	Common Pain Points	What They Care About	How to Tailor Your Pitch
D2C eCommerce	High CAC, low retention, cart abandonment	ROAS, LTV, repeat customers, creative fatigue	Talk about CRO, email flows, upsells, AOV increase
SaaS	Low trial-to-paid conversion, churn, noisy leads	MRR, activation rate, product onboarding	Focus on funnel alignment, paid + product-led growth
EdTech	Low lead quality, cost of student acquisition	CPL, conversion to enrollment, credibility	Talk lead scoring, remarketing, trust-building content
IT Services	Lack of quality leads, weak positioning	Global credibility, sales velocity, referrals	Highlight positioning strategy, warm outreach, SDRs
HR Tech	Low demo bookings, vague messaging	Qualified leads, better targeting, short sales cycle	Emphasize precision targeting and use case clarity
Fintech	Compliance, low trust, long sales cycle	Lead quality, data security, conversion funnel	Focus on trust-building ads, short-form signups
Healthcare/Wellness	Low awareness, regulatory hurdles	Local lead gen, education, cost-efficiency	Use educational content, performance tracking

Industry-Based Personalization

? Example: Comfroi Pitch to a D2C vs. SaaS Brand

? Pitching Performance Partnership Model

To a D2C skincare brand in Sydney:

"Your returning customer rate is 16%. Industry benchmark is 28%. We help brands fix that using better email flows and post-purchase touchpoints."

To a SaaS tool in the UK:

"Let's increase trial-to-paid conversions by improving onboarding journeys and integrating retargeting across LinkedIn + email."

? The magic?

We spoke their business language, not agency talk.

? 3. Company/Stage-Based Personalization

Startups and enterprises have different pain points:

Stage	What They Need	Pitch Focus
Startup	Speed, flexibility, lean team support	Talk agility, MVP mindset, founder involvement
Scale-Up	Process, reporting, results	Talk dashboards, playbooks, scalable systems
Enterprise	Governance, risk reduction, consistency	Talk SOPs, case studies, large-scale deployment

Company/Stage-Based Personalization

? Example: Perfozi Pitch to Two Ahmedabad Firms

? Company 1: 10-member IT startup

Pitch:

"We'll find you a sales rep and coach them weekly—so you're not babysitting or spending hours training. You stay focused on building."

? Company 2: 300-employee established tech firm

Pitch:

"You get a sales resource who plugs into your CRM, works off our scorecard, and reports weekly performance—tracked against KPIs set by your managers."

? Both said yes.

Because both felt like our pitch matched their reality.

? How to Personalize Quickly (Without Burning Hours)

You don't need a 3-day research project. Here's a 5-minute framework I teach in my workshops:

➡? Vikas Jain's Quick Pitch-Personalization Framework

Step	Question	Example
1. Who's the buyer?	Role/title	"Founder or CMO?"
2. What do they care about?	Top KPI	"Revenue? CPL? Hiring success?"
3. What do they fear?	Unspoken worry	"Wasted spend? Team burnout?"
4. What proof can I show?	Case study match	"Have we helped a similar client?"
5. What's the *one sentence* that will hit home?	Custom opener	"Saw your LinkedIn post about scaling—can I share something that might help?"

Vikas Jain's Quick Pitch-Personalization Framework

? Advanced Tip: Mirror Their Language

Psychological Insight:

According to Neurolinguistic Programming (NLP), people trust those who speak their language—literally.

Use the words your buyer uses:

- **If they say "users," don't say "customers."**
- **If they say "pipeline," don't say "lead flow."**

· **If they say "team burnout," don't say "productivity drop."**

This creates subconscious alignment and builds trust without trying too hard.

? *Real-Time Customization on Calls*

If you're on a live video call and discover something mid-conversation, pivot your pitch in real time.

? *Example: Perfozi Call with HR + Founder (Ahmedabad)*

I was pitching a trained SDR for outbound prospecting.
Halfway through, the founder said:
"Actually, we're thinking of shifting focus to inbound qualification."
Immediately, I flipped the pitch:
"That's perfect. The rep we've shortlisted has worked on inbound lead scoring and objection handling in HubSpot. Would you like to meet her?"
We secured the deal because we didn't stick to a script—we responded like a partner.

? *Final Thought:*

The closer your pitch feels to their context, the closer you are to a "yes."
Personalization isn't about adding their name to the email.
It's about showing them, line by line, slide by slide, that you understand what they need—often better than they do.
In the next chapter, we'll explore how to handle objections—not with resistance, but with strategy, empathy, and confidence.
Because the best salespeople don't fight objections—they welcome them.
— Vikas Jain

SEVEN

BUILDING TRUST WITH DATA AND CREDIBILITY

In today's hyper-informed world, even the most charming salesperson can't close deals on charisma alone. Buyers expect proof.

They need evidence to trust you.

"Storytelling wins attention. Data wins trust."

— Vikas Jain

When you skillfully combine stories + data + social proof, you stop being just another vendor—you become a trusted advisor.

This chapter will show you exactly how to do that—and how I personally used these techniques to close some of the biggest deals at Marastu, Comfroi, and Perfozi.

? Why Data and Credibility Matter in Sales

Psychological Insight:

The Cognitive Trust Model says that humans trust faster when two conditions are met:

- **Warmth (empathy, listening)**
- **Competence (proof, results)**

- **Warmth gets you attention.**
- **Competence wins the deal.**

And credibility (testimonials, case studies, numbers) is your strongest tool to demonstrate competence without bragging.

? Blending Storytelling with Stats and Testimonials

Don't just tell a story. Anchor it in numbers.
Don't just show numbers. Wrap them in a story.
Here's how to blend both:

? Real-World Example: Marastu Pitch to a SaaS Platform in the UK

The Story:

"When we first started working with a SaaS platform similar to yours, they were stuck at a 1.2% MQL-to-SQL conversion rate."

The Stats:

"In 90 days, after aligning paid and organic messaging, we brought it up to 3.8%—a 216% improvement."

The Testimonial:

"Their CMO said working with us felt like 'having a performance engine plugged into their marketing team.'"

Result:

We closed a 12-month retainer with the new client after one follow-up call.

Framework for Blending:

- **Start with a relatable problem story.**
- **Share a real, verifiable data outcome.**
- **Seal it with a quote or testimonial.**

When you do this, you engage both the emotional and rational sides of the buyer's brain.

? *Using Social Proof Effectively*

Not all social proof is created equal.
The key to effective proof is relevance.

Type of Social Proof	When to Use	Example
Customer Testimonial	Early stage (build trust)	"A founder just like you saw X result with us."
Case Study	Mid-funnel (overcome objections)	"Here's a real-world example of what we achieved."
Ratings & Awards	Late stage (reassure decision)	"We're rated Top 5 in [industry platform]."
Logos/Clients Served	Early stage (credibility signal)	"Brands like [XYZ] trust us too."

Using Social Proof Effectively

? *Example: Comfroi Pitch to an Australian D2C Brand*

While pitching our Performance Partnership Model (PPM), the founder said:
"How do I know you'll actually deliver and not just promise like every other agency?"
Instead of arguing, I shared:
A case study of a Melbourne fashion brand we helped grow revenue by 3x.
A 30-second video testimonial from their founder.
Screenshots of Shopify revenue analytics (with client permission).

The result?

He replied:

"If they trusted you—and you delivered—I'm comfortable moving forward."

Lesson:

People trust other buyers more than they trust sellers.

? *Common Objections by Industry—and How to Overcome Them with Confidence*

Every industry has recurring doubts.
Here's how I teach teams to preempt and address them confidently:

Industry	Common Objection	How to Overcome with Credibility
D2C eCommerce	"How can I trust you'll improve my ROI?"	Show case studies with real before/after ROAS and customer retention numbers.
SaaS	"Will your leads actually convert?"	Share funnel-specific conversion improvements (MQL to SQL) and testimonials.
EdTech	"Are your leads high quality or junk?"	Share CPL benchmarks, lead scoring models, and enrollment conversion stats.
IT Services	"We tried marketing before; it failed."	Show a case study of a similar IT company and focus on your process improvements (not promises).
HR Tech	"How will you qualify candidates?"	Share screening frameworks, example scorecards, and weekly coaching success stories.
Fintech	"Is it safe and compliant?"	Show your compliance checklist, lead generation protocols, and references from similar sectors.
Healthcare	"Are you experienced with healthcare regulations?"	Share examples of HIPAA/GDPR-compliant marketing or content strategies you executed.

Common Objections by Industry—and How to Overcome Them with Confidence

? *Psychological Triggers Used in Objection Handling:*

Trigger	How it Helps
Risk Reversal	Reduces fear by offering trials, guarantees, or pay-for-performance models.
Authority Bias	Quotes from respected clients or certifications make you seem more credible.
Scarcity	Subtle mentions ("We take on only 2-3 new clients per month") create urgency.
Proof Over Promise	Showing real screenshots/testimonials is 10x more powerful than promising results verbally.

Psychological Triggers Used in Objection Handling

? *Real-World Example: Perfozi Pitch to an Ahmedabad-Based IT Company*

When an Ahmedabad-based SaaS startup said:

"We already hired salespeople before and none of them performed. Why should Perfozi be different?"

Instead of selling harder, I calmly replied:

"You're right to be skeptical. Many companies face that.

Here's what we changed for a similar startup:

Weekly SDR performance reviews (sample dashboard shown)

Personal coaching sessions (calendar screenshots)

SLA on minimum meeting counts (client testimonial shown)

Within 60 days, they doubled their weekly qualified meetings."

Result:

Trust rebuilt. Objection neutralized. Deal closed.

? *Final Thought:*

"Data earns you the right to tell a story.
Stories give your data meaning.
Together, they earn you trust—and trust closes deals."

— Vikas Jain

When you blend the head (data) with the heart (stories), your pitch becomes not just persuasive—but undeniable.

In the next chapter, we'll explore how to handle real objections live on the call—not just with scripts, but with confidence, strategic listening, and framing techniques.

Because in modern sales, objection handling isn't the end of the deal—it's the beginning of trust.

— Vikas Jain

EIGHT

HANDLING OBJECTIONS WITH STRATEGIC CONFIDENCE

"An objection is not a rejection. It's an invitation—to go deeper."
— Vikas Jain

In the world of modern sales, objections are inevitable.
And that's a good thing.

Because an objection means:

- **The buyer is thinking seriously.**
- **The buyer sees potential but has concerns.**
- **You have an opening to build deeper trust.**

But only if you handle it strategically, empathetically, and confidently.

? Why Objections Happen (Buyer Psychology)

Objections aren't logical barriers—they're emotional reactions driven by fear and risk aversion.

Here are the real reasons behind most objections:

Emotional Fear	How It Shows Up as an Objection
Fear of loss	"What if this doesn't work?"
Fear of embarrassment	"What if I recommend you and it fails?"
Fear of wasting time	"I'm not sure it's the right priority now."
Fear of financial risk	"It's too expensive."

Why Objections Happen (Buyer Psychology)

When you respond to an objection, you're not fighting the words—you're soothing the emotion behind them.

? Golden Rule: Don't Argue. Align and Redirect.

- **Acknowledge their concern (build empathy)**
- **Align your understanding with theirs (build trust)**
- **Redirect to a new, safer frame (reduce fear)**

? Vikas Jain's Strategic Objection Handling Formula

3 Steps:

- **Validate — "That's a very valid point..."**
- **Relate — "In fact, another client felt the same way..."**
- **Resolve — "Here's what we did and why it worked."**

This diffuses defensiveness and builds momentum instead of confrontation.

? *Real-World Example: Marastu Video Call with a Fintech Startup (USA)*

Objection:

"We're worried we'll spend on ads and still not see real pipeline movement."

My Response (Vikas Jain):

Validate —
"You're absolutely right to be cautious, especially in Fintech where pipeline health is everything."
Relate —
"Another founder I worked with had exactly the same concern after losing money with two agencies."
Resolve —
"We solved it by mapping attribution in real time—so every $ spent could be tied to an actual SQL, not just impressions. Happy to show you a live dashboard if you like."

? *Result:*

Trust rebuilt. They invited us for a second call with their CRO.

? *"Magic Phrases" That Calm Buyers Instantly*

Here are phrases you can memorize and deploy during tough moments:

Magic Phrase	When to Use
"That's a smart question—I'm glad you brought it up."	When facing skepticism
"If I were in your shoes, I'd be asking the same thing."	When facing resistance
"Would it help if I showed you exactly how we handled this for another client?"	When facing doubt
"No pressure at all—only if it feels like a fit after we walk through it."	When buyer hesitates to commit
"What would make you feel 100% comfortable moving forward?"	When you want to surface hidden objections

Magic Phrases" That Calm Buyers Instantly

? Common Industry-Based Objections (and How I Handle Them)

Industry	Typical Objection	Strategic Response
D2C eCommerce	"What if your campaigns don't drive sales?"	"Great question. We work on a pay-for-performance model—our growth is tied to yours. Let's set specific KPIs upfront."
SaaS	"Will your leads actually convert?"	"Fair concern. Our process includes lead scoring before handing them off to Sales. I can share examples."
IT Services	"Our market is too competitive."	"Exactly why messaging clarity matters more than just spend. I can show you how we positioned a similar IT client successfully."
HR Tech	"We've had bad experiences with other recruiters."	"Completely understandable. That's why we provide weekly performance reports—not just placements."
Fintech	"Compliance is a big risk."	"Absolutely. We follow GDPR and regulatory-safe ad practices, and we can walk you through our compliance checklist."

Common Industry-Based Objections (and How I Handle Them)

? Real Live Examples of Vikas Handling Objections

? Perfozi Video Call with an Ahmedabad SaaS Firm

Objection:

"We're not sure remote SDRs will understand US clients well enough."
My Live Response:
Validate:
"That's a valid concern—communication quality makes or breaks outbound sales."
Relate:
"Another SaaS founder in Ahmedabad had the same hesitation initially."
Resolve:
"We fixed it by training SDRs in cultural nuance roleplays, and we provide you with sample call recordings weekly to monitor. Would you like me to send you a real example?"
? Outcome:
The founder said:
"If you're already running these drills, that's impressive."
He signed a 3-month trial with Perfozi.

? Comfroi Video Call with an Australian Retail Brand

Objection:
"We're not sure if the performance model is too risky for you."
My Response:
"It actually reduces your risk—we only grow when you do."
"We define success metrics together before any commitment."
Result:
Founder said:
"This feels more like a partnership than a gamble."
We closed the deal.

? Psychological Techniques Embedded:

Technique	What It Does
Risk Reversal	Shifts perceived risk back onto you, making you seem confident.
Social Proof Relating	Makes the buyer feel they aren't alone in their doubts.
Future Pacing	Gets buyers visualizing success after solving their objection.
Empathy Anchoring	Disarms defensiveness and makes the buyer feel respected.

Psychological Techniques Embedded:

? Final Thought

**"The strongest salespeople don't defeat objections.
They defuse fears, build bridges, and invite trust."
— Vikas Jain**

When you shift your mindset from defending your pitch to defending the buyer's future success, objections become your greatest ally—not your enemy.

In the next chapter, we'll explore how to close deals naturally—by creating irresistible next steps that feel less like a "hard close" and more like a mutual agreement.

Because in modern sales, the best closing techniques are those that feel effortless, obvious, and collaborative.

Let's learn how to close the right way.

— Vikas Jain

NINE

Closing the Deal Without "Hard Selling"

"The best closes don't feel like closes—they feel like natural next steps."
— Vikas Jain

The old-school "hard sell" is dead.

Today, closing a deal is not about pressure—it's about creating clarity, building confidence, and making the next step feel obvious.

In this chapter, I'll show you exactly how to close deals naturally, perfect your pitch timing, respect the buyer's time, and refine your skills continuously—based on real methods I use at Marastu, Comfroi, and Perfozi.

? *The Psychology of Closing Without Pressure*

Buyer Mindset at Decision Stage:

- **They want to feel in control.**
- **They want to justify the decision internally (to themselves and/or their team).**
- **They fear regret or making a mistake.**

The role of a great closer is not to push harder, but to make the buyer feel safe moving forward.

"The smoother your closing feels, the stronger your positioning becomes."

? How to Close Without Hard Selling: Vikas Jain's 4-Step Framework

Summarize the journey
("Here's what we discussed, and why it matters...")
   Frame the vision
("Imagine starting with X results in Y days...")
   Offer the next step—not the final step
("How about we set up an onboarding call to get you familiar with the process? No commitment today.")
   Give them a clear, no-pressure exit
("If it feels right, we move ahead. If not, no worries at all.")

? Magic Closing Phrases That Don't Feel "Salesy"

Phrase	Purpose
"Would you like me to send a simple next-step plan?"	Creates clarity
"What would make this a 100% yes for you?"	Surfaces hidden doubts
"Would you feel comfortable if we penciled a kickoff call?"	Low-pressure assumption
"I want this to be a win-win. If it's not the right fit, that's completely fine too."	Removes defensiveness

Magic Closing Phrases That Don't Feel "Salesy"

? Perfecting Pitch Length for Emails, Calls, and Presentations

One of the most underrated secrets to closing is respecting the buyer's time.
Long-winded pitches feel desperate.
Crisp pitches feel powerful and confident.
   Here's how I coach sales teams to optimize pitch length:

Channel	Ideal Length	Why It Matters
Emails	Under 200 words	Buyers skim. Short emails = Higher replies.
Calls	7–12 minutes max for discovery calls	Keeps energy high. Forces focus on essentials.
Presentations	Max 15-18 minutes	TED Talks are 18 minutes for a reason—attention spans drop after that.

Perfecting Pitch Length for Emails, Calls, and Presentations

? *Example: Marastu Cold Email That Landed a US SaaS Client*

3 short paragraphs
  Personalized first line
  One clear CTA ("Would you be open to a 15-min call?")
  Result:
Booked a meeting in 2 hours.
  Tip: In cold emails, every extra sentence must earn its place.

? *Example: Perfozi Video Discovery Call (Ahmedabad IT Firm)*

2 min intro
  6 min diagnosis of their sales hiring challenges
  3 min value proposition
  2 min CTA
  Result:
Founder said:
  "You respected my time—and my brain."
  We closed the trial on the spot.

⌛ *Strategies to Respect Your Audience's Time*

Agenda upfront ("We'll cover 3 quick points today—problem, solution, next steps.")

Check-in halfway ("Are we on track so far?")

Offer to skip ("I can fast-forward this part if you're already familiar.")

Timebox commitment ("This will take no more than 12 minutes, I promise.")

Respecting time builds trust faster than overloading people with information.

? Recording, Reviewing, and Refining Your Pitch

Top sales performers treat pitching like professional athletes treat game film.

At Marastu and Perfozi, I make recording pitches mandatory during training cycles.

Here's the system I use:

? Vikas Jain's Pitch Review Process:

- **Record every important pitch (Zoom, Meet, phone).**
- **Review within 24 hours—alone or with a coach.**
- **Score yourself on:**
- **Hook strength**
- **Relevance to buyer pain**
- **Handling objections naturally**
- **Clear call-to-action**

Identify 1 tweak to improve for next time (not 10 things—just 1).

? Real Example: Comfroi Internal Pitch Review

After a pitch review session, I spotted:

Too much time spent on agency credentials

Not enough time connecting to the client's new product launch timeline

We changed our structure to open every call by connecting to the client's timing goals first.

Result:
Our close rate increased by 18% in the next 30 days.
Lesson:
Small refinements = Big impact over time.

? Role-Playing Exercises and Scenarios

Practice like you pitch.

At Perfozi, every sales trainee goes through roleplay rounds before touching real prospects.

Here's how we structure it:

Roleplay Type	Focus
High-Skeptic Prospect	Handling hard objections with empathy
Short-Call Challenge	Deliver value in under 5 minutes
Lost Prospect Recovery	Re-pitching a cold/lost lead with fresh framing
Multiple Stakeholders	Handling 2–3 different role-based objections in one call

Role-Playing Exercises and Scenarios

??♂? Quick Roleplay Drill You Can Try:

Partner up with a colleague.

1. One plays a skeptical CFO.
2. One plays the seller.
3. Switch after 5 minutes.
4. Record both sessions.

Debrief:

1. Where did trust build?

2. Where did energy dip?
3. Was the CTA clear?

Do this 2-3 times a week—and your live closing skills will skyrocket.

? Final Thought:

"Closing isn't about winning.
It's about making the buyer feel they've already won."
— Vikas Jain

When you master respectful timing, strategic clarity, and confident closing, you won't need to "sell" at all.

Buyers will feel relieved to say yes—because it will feel like the natural, intelligent, inevitable next step.

In the next chapter, we'll explore what to do after you close—how to onboard, set expectations, and turn new customers into raving advocates.

Because winning the deal is just the beginning.

— Vikas Jain

TEN
Post-Sale Mastery—Turning Clients into Champions

"A closed deal is not the finish line—it's the starting point of building a legacy."
— Vikas Jain

Winning a client is exciting.

But keeping a client—and turning them into a raving advocate—is where real growth happens.

In fact, studies show:

It costs 5x more to acquire a new customer than to retain an existing one.

Loyal customers are 4x more likely to refer new business.

Testimonials from real clients increase close rates by up to 34%.

In this chapter, I'll walk you through how to master the post-sale journey—the part most salespeople and businesses neglect—and why doing it right has been a game-changer for Marastu, Comfroi, and Perfozi.

? Why Post-Sale Matters

Psychological Insight:

- **The Peak-End Rule states that people judge an experience based largely on:**
- **The most intense moment**
- **The final moments (the ending)**

This means:

How you onboard and deliver in the first 30-60 days defines your client's long-term memory of you.

If you "wow" them early, you create emotional loyalty that no competitor can easily break.

? *Step 1: Celebrate the Win Together*

When a client signs up, don't just say "thanks."

Mark the moment.

? *Real Example: Marastu Client Win*

After closing a big SEO retainer with a Fintech client in the US, we:

Sent a customized welcome email with their logo

Shared a LinkedIn post celebrating the partnership (tagging them)

Booked a "Kickoff Success Workshop" instead of a boring "Onboarding Call"

Result:

They felt valued, respected, and publicly recognized before we even delivered results.

Lesson:

Treat Day 1 like a mini-success—not like paperwork.

? *Step 2: Set Clear, Mutual Expectations*

"Disappointment happens when reality doesn't match expectation."

Right after the deal closes:

- **Clarify deliverables**
- **Set milestones**
- **Define responsibilities (yours and theirs)**
- **Set reporting frequency**

? Example: Comfroi Onboarding Document

When onboarding a D2C client:
    We define ROAS targets
    Clarify ad budgets
    Set creative revision policies
    Share a 90-day roadmap
    Clients love it because it eliminates confusion early.
    Pro Tip:
Always ask:
    "What would make you feel we're making great progress after 30 days?"
    Capture their emotional metric—not just project goals.

? Step 3: Deliver Early Wins

Momentum is powerful.
    Your goal should be:
Deliver small, visible wins in the first 30-45 days—even if the full result takes longer.

? Real Example: Comfroi for an Australian Fashion Brand

Instead of focusing first on complicated CRO tests, we:
    Optimized 5 top-selling products' landing pages immediately
    Launched remarketing ads to repeat customers
    Within 20 days:
    Email open rates jumped by 15%
    Returning customer rate increased by 8%

? We celebrated these wins even before scaling ads.

Result:
The client felt energized—and referred us to two more brands in their network.
    Lesson:
Small early wins = Massive emotional trust.

? Step 4: Over-Communicate Progress (Even If There's No Big News)

Never make your client wonder what's happening.
Set a rhythm for communication:

- **Weekly updates (even if it's just a check-in)**
- **Monthly review calls**
- **Quarterly strategy resets**

At Perfozi, our SDR placement clients get:

- **Weekly performance emails**
- **Fortnightly live coaching session recaps**
- **Quarterly review call on pipeline movement**

Tip:
Even if there's no huge update, report on effort + next steps.
Clients value proactive transparency more than constant big wins.

? Step 5: Turn Happy Clients into Advocates

Once you've delivered visible value:
Ask for testimonials while the momentum is high.
Request referrals naturally (after key success milestones).
Invite them to be part of your marketing (case studies, webinars, etc.).
Don't be shy.
If you've truly helped them, most will happily support you.

? Example: How Marastu Got a Key Referral

After helping a New York SaaS company double their MQL-to-SQL rate in 90 days:
We asked for a video testimonial (they agreed happily).
We sent them a "Congrats" gift pack when they hit their ARR goal.
One month later, they referred us to two VC-funded startups from their founder network.
? That referral alone led to $140,000 in annual revenue.

? *Checklist: Turning New Clients into Champions*

Roleplay Type	Focus
High-Skeptic Prospect	Handling hard objections with empathy
Short-Call Challenge	Deliver value in under 5 minutes
Lost Prospect Recovery	Re-pitching a cold/lost lead with fresh framing
Multiple Stakeholders	Handling 2–3 different role-based objections in one call

Checklist: Turning New Clients into Champions

? *Final Thought:*

"Selling starts the relationship. Serving grows it. Surprising and delighting cements it for life."
— Vikas Jain

If you want exponential growth, focus not just on closing clients—focus on transforming clients into your most vocal champions.

Because in today's world, word-of-mouth isn't just marketing—

It's your moat. It's your momentum. It's your mission.

— Vikas Jain

ELEVEN

THE ART OF THE FOLLOW-UP

**"Most deals aren't lost because of the first conversation.
They're lost because** the follow-up was weak—or non-existent."
— Vikas Jain

You can deliver a flawless pitch.

You can handle objections with elegance.

You can even feel like the meeting went great.

And still lose the deal—if you don't master the art of the follow-up.

In today's hyper-distracted world, the real money isn't made at the first touch—it's made through thoughtful, strategic, value-driven follow-ups.

This chapter will show you why most follow-ups fail, how to fix them, and how I (Vikas Jain) coach sales teams at Marastu, Comfroi, and Perfozi to build winning follow-up systems.

? Why Most Follow-Ups Fail

Most follow-ups are either:

Too passive ("Just checking in...")

Too aggressive ("Any update? I'm waiting.")

Too generic ("Let me know if you have questions.")

The problem?

They add no new value to the conversation.

If your follow-up doesn't move the buyer closer to a decision—or at least deepen their trust—you're wasting their attention.

? Vikas Jain's Definition of a Great Follow-Up:

"A follow-up should either add insight, reduce risk, or make the next step easier."

If it does none of these, don't send it.

? Psychological Insight: Buyer Behavior Post-Call

After a sales call, buyers typically go through:

Excitement Phase (first 24 hours)
→ They're still emotionally connected.
Doubt Phase (days 2–5)
→ Other priorities kick in. Skepticism creeps in.
Decision Fatigue Phase (after day 5)
→ If not reminded or re-engaged, they mentally "close the file."
Timing and relevance are everything.

? Strategies for Value-Driven Follow-Ups

Here's how to follow up like a pro—and not sound like everyone else:

Roleplay Type	Focus
High-Skeptic Prospect	Handling hard objections with empathy
Short-Call Challenge	Deliver value in under 5 minutes
Lost Prospect Recovery	Re-pitching a cold/lost lead with fresh framing
Multiple Stakeholders	Handling 2–3 different role-based objections in one call

Strategies for Value-Driven Follow-Ups

? Real Example: Marastu Follow-Up That Won a Retainer

After a discovery call with a Fintech client in the US, instead of a boring "just checking in" email, I sent:

- A simple 3-point strategy doc
- A case study from a similar B2B Fintech firm
- A suggestion for a quick "next-step mapping" call

Subject line:
"Your Growth Plan | 3 Moves in 90 Days"
Result:
They booked a second meeting immediately—and signed a 6-month contract within two weeks.

? Vikas's Recommended Follow-Up Tools

Over time, I realized that traditional emails often weren't enough, especially for larger B2B deals. So I started using strategic tools like:

1. Digital Sales Rooms

A Digital Sales Room is a personalized, private link you send to the prospect. It includes:

A recording of your discovery/pitch call

Tailored case studies

Product/service brochures

Testimonials

Pricing sheets

A next-step button (e.g., "Book a follow-up")

Why it works:

It feels organized, personal, and allows the prospect to revisit and share internally at their convenience.

At Comfroi, this strategy helped us close a Melbourne-based apparel client by giving their co-founders a shared resource to review at their own pace.

2. Tailored Case Studies and Proof Packs

Instead of a "one size fits all" deck, I send:

A customized 1-page case study

Specific performance stats matching their business model

A short quote/testimonial from a similar client

At Perfozi, for example, when we pitched an SDR placement to an Ahmedabad SaaS firm, we shared:

A success story of an SDR placed in a similar-sized tech company

Weekly call sheet samples

Sample KPI tracking sheets

Result:

It made the client feel like we had already "been there, done that" successfully.

3. Strategic Content Sharing

Sometimes, I simply send:

- **A video breakdown (2–3 minutes) summarizing the key opportunity**
- **An industry article or research that strengthens our solution's importance**
- **A checklist or framework that makes decision-making easier**

Tip:

Sharing something valuable—even before closing—shows confidence and abundance, not desperation.

? Vikas Jain's 5-Day Follow-Up Framework

Day	Action
Day 1	Send a recap + next-step proposal
Day 3	Share tailored case study or proof pack
Day 5	Share new insight or helpful content
Day 7	Light nudge: "Still open to exploring this?"
Day 10+	Close the loop respectfully if no response: "Happy to reconnect when the timing is better."

Vikas Jain's 5-Day Follow-Up Framework

Consistency builds credibility.

Buyers don't mind multiple touchpoints if each one adds value, not

pressure.

? *Final Thought:*

"**Great follow-ups aren't reminders—they're reinforcements of your value.**"
— Vikas Jain

If your follow-ups make the prospect smarter, safer, or more certain—you'll always stay top of mind.

And when the moment comes to make a decision, you won't be one of many vendors...

You'll be the obvious partner.

In the final chapter, we'll wrap it all together:

Real-World Pitch Examples by Scenario

And how to position yourself as a sales professional clients love working with.

Because pitching, closing, and following up are just the beginning of a truly successful sales career.

— Vikas Jain

TWELVE

REAL-WORLD PITCH EXAMPLES BY SCENARIO

"The right pitch at the wrong time—or through the wrong channel—is still the wrong pitch."
— Vikas Jain

You've now learned the art and science behind crafting a perfect sales pitch.

But one critical factor remains: Adapting your pitch to the channel you're using.

Because pitching over the phone is very different from pitching over email.

An elevator pitch is even tighter.

A website pitch must convert without you even being present.

In this chapter, I'll walk you through real-world examples of how I (Vikas Jain) and my teams at Marastu, Comfroi, and Perfozi craft channel-specific pitches that work—and why.

? Why Different Channels Need Different Pitches

Psychological Insight:

Each communication channel affects attention span, context, and decision-making speed.

Channel	Buyer Mindset		What Your Pitch Must Do
Phone Call	Distracted, multitasking		Grab attention fast, drive curiosity
Email	Skimming, short attention span		Be concise, valuable, easy to respond
Elevator	Limited time, zero patience		Create curiosity + desire in < 60 seconds
Website	Self-paced, skeptical, comparing options		Build immediate trust, showcase proof, offer next step

Why Different Channels Need Different Pitches

? Phone Pitch Breakdown

? Goal:

Capture attention fast, create relevance, secure a next step (not close the deal immediately).

? Real Example: Marastu Phone Pitch to a UK SaaS Startup

Call Opening (within 10 seconds):
    "Hi [Name], this is Vikas from Marastu.
I'll be super quick—
I noticed your team's been actively hiring SDRs.
We recently helped a similar SaaS company increase lead-to-demo conversion by 40% through better paid campaign alignment.
Would you be open to a quick 15-minute conversation later this week to explore?"
    Why It Works:

- **Personalized**
- **Specific result stated**
- **Low-pressure ask**
- **Shows respect for time**

? Email Pitch Breakdown

? Goal:

Spark curiosity, highlight a specific benefit, invite a low-commitment next step.

? Real Example: Comfroi Cold Email to an Australian D2C Brand

Subject:

"Boost Your Returning Customer Rate by 20% in 90 Days"

Body:

Hi [Name],

Noticed [Brand] is doing some fantastic work with [Product line]!

I specialize in helping D2C brands like yours turn first-time buyers into loyal customers—without heavy discounting.

Example: Helped a Melbourne brand grow their returning customer rate by 22% in under 3 months through smarter retargeting and loyalty flows.

Would love to share a few quick ideas—would 15 minutes next week work for you?

Cheers,

Vikas

Why It Works:

- **Personalization at the start (emotional hook)**
- **Specific, measurable result**
- **Clear CTA with low pressure ("quick ideas")**

? Elevator Pitch Breakdown

? Goal:

Convey value proposition under 60 seconds so the prospect says:
"Tell me more."

? Real Example: Perfozi Elevator Pitch to an Investor at a Networking Event

Pitch:
"Most companies hire salespeople based on interviews—and gamble on whether they perform.
At Perfozi, we place trained SDRs with built-in performance coaching, KPIs, and weekly tracking.
You don't hire talent—you hire guaranteed output."
Duration:
? Under 40 seconds.
Result:
Immediate investor interest → Follow-up meeting booked.

? Website Pitch Breakdown

? Goal:
Build trust fast, create emotional resonance, offer clear micro-conversions.

? Real Example: Comfroi Website Hero Section

Headline:
"We Grow Your Shopify Store. We Only Win When You Win."
Sub-Headline:
"Performance marketing, growth strategy, and CRO for D2C brands—backed by a pay-for-results model. No retainers. No wasted spend."
Call-to-Action Buttons:
"Book a Free Strategy Call"
"See Our Client Success Stories"
Why It Works:

- **Value proposition instantly clear**
- **Risk reversal ("We only win when you do")**
- **Immediate next actions offered**

? Best Practices for Pitches Across All Channels

Best Practice	Why It Matters
Personalize Fast	Shows relevance and earns attention immediately
Focus on One Key Benefit	Simplicity beats complexity
Use Social Proof	Build trust even in short formats
Always Have a CTA	Never leave them wondering "what's next?"
Respect Time	Short, sharp, and impactful wins the day

Best Practices for Pitches Across All Channels

? *Final Thought:*

"Adaptability in your pitch is just as important as the pitch itself."
— Vikas Jain

The way you pitch over a phone, an email, an elevator ride, or a website must change based on context, attention span, and psychology.

Master these different forms—and you'll never be "pushing" again.

You'll be inviting buyers to lean in—naturally, effortlessly, and repeatedly.

THIRTEEN

Epilogue: Your Journey to Perfecting the Pitch

When I first started my career in sales, like many of you, I believed that a perfect pitch was about dazzling the prospect—sounding polished, reciting stats, having the right slides.

But over the years—and across thousands of pitches, closed deals, lost deals, recovered deals, and lasting relationships—I learned something far more powerful:

The perfect pitch is not a performance. It's a connection.

It's the moment when your prospect feels:

"You understand me better than I understand myself."

It's not about selling.

- **It's about serving.**
- **It's not about pressure.**
- **It's about clarity.**
- **It's not about "winning" the conversation.**
- **It's about creating certainty for the buyer—and sometimes, even for yourself.**

? *Your True Mission as a Seller*

Every pitch you craft from today onward is not just a way to close a deal.
It's an opportunity to:

- **Solve real problems**
- **Empower real people**
- **Build real partnerships**
- **Leave a lasting impact on someone's business—and life**

Sales isn't about moving products.
It's about moving people toward a better future—with you by their side.

? *Your Next Steps*

As you close this book, I want to leave you with a challenge:
Don't just read these frameworks—practice them.

- **Personalize your next email.**
- **Rewrite your next discovery call agenda to focus on them, not you.**
- **Create a mini customer story for your next follow-up.**
- **Send a value-driven piece of content before your next meeting.**
- **Role-play objection handling with a friend or teammate.**
- **Record and review your next pitch call—not to criticize yourself, but to coach yourself.**

Every pitch you give is a seed planted.
Some seeds will grow immediately.
Some will need time and nurturing.
But every seed, if planted thoughtfully, expands your reputation, your network, your opportunities, and your impact.

? *Final Thought from Vikas Jain*

**"The world doesn't need another slick salesperson.
It needs trusted advisors. Problem solvers. Partners who care.
Be that person—and your success will be inevitable."**

Thank you for joining me on this journey.

Now go out there, craft your perfect pitches—not by chasing perfection, but by embracing connection.

And remember:

A truly perfect pitch isn't one that sounds great.

It's one that feels right—to the person hearing it.

Your best pitches—and your best career moments—are still ahead of you.

Let's create them, one conversation at a time.

— Vikas Jain

? Stay Connected

If you found this book valuable, I would love to hear about your journey!

Connect with me:

LinkedIn: https://www.linkedin.com/in/digitalevangelist-monks/

Website: Perfozi.com, Marastu.com, Comfroi.com

Email: vikasjain1979@gmail.com

I also invite you to explore deeper training, pitch templates, live role-playing sessions, and mentoring opportunities through my consulting brands: Marastu™, Comfroi, and Perfozi.

This is just the beginning. Let's build greatness together.

A Big Thank You!

Vikas Krishna Kumar Jain

Precision Persona Strategy (pps) — The Hidden Engine Behind Every Great Pitch

"If you don't know exactly who you're speaking to—and what they care about—you're not pitching.
You're guessing."
— Vikas Jain

Every sales leader talks about "understanding your customer."
Few teach you how to actually do it at the pitch level.

After years of helping businesses across the US, UK, Australia, and India close high-value deals at Marastu™, Comfroi™, and Perfozi™, I realized that most sales pitches fail not because of weak delivery, but because of vague targeting.

That's why I developed the Precision Persona Strategy (PPS)—a simple, powerful framework that ensures every pitch lands exactly where it needs to.

In this chapter, I'll break it down fully—so you can use it to transform your pitches starting today.

? What Is the Precision Persona Strategy (PPS)?

The Precision Persona Strategy is a systematic method for identifying, understanding, and speaking directly to the real emotional and business needs of your target buyer.

Rather than pitching to a "company" or "title," PPS makes you pitch to a living, breathing human being—with goals, fears, biases, and aspirations.

When you align your pitch perfectly to that buyer's persona, the deal becomes not about pushing—

It becomes about guiding them home to the solution they already want.

? The 4 Pillars of Precision Persona Strategy

Pillar	Description	Your Objective
1. Profile	Identify WHO exactly you are pitching to.	Clarify the buyer role and emotional drivers.
2. Pain	Understand the problems THEY are actively aware of.	Speak their pain better than they can.
3. Priority	Know what matters MOST to them *right now*.	Align your pitch to their current goals, not general benefits.
4. Proof	Prepare proof relevant to THEIR world.	Use stories, case studies, and metrics they'll care about.

The 4 Pillars of Precision Persona Strategy

? *Step-by-Step: How to Use PPS in Your Pitches*

1. *Profile the Buyer (Beyond the Title)*

Don't just know they are a "CMO" or "Founder."
Understand:

- **Their career path (check LinkedIn)**
- **Their priorities (check their posts, company news)**
- **Their biases (startups value agility; corporates value risk reduction)**
- **Their personal KPIs (lead volume? cost cutting? market share?)**

? *Example: Comfroi Pitch to a Retail Founder in Australia*

Title: Founder
 Profile Insight:
Loves innovation but hates complex marketing jargon.
 Pitch Adjustment:
Focused on simple outcome promises ("More orders, fewer marketing headaches").
 2. Define the Buyer's Pain Points

Not "what your product does," but "what problem it solves for THEM."
Common pain categories:

- **Inefficiency**
- **Revenue stagnation**
- **Operational chaos**
- **Employee churn**
- **Risk of falling behind competitors**

? Example: Marastu SaaS Pitch in the UK

Pain point discovered:
Huge marketing budget → Poor MQL-to-SQL conversion.
Pitch Framing:
Not "better ads."
Instead:
"Higher-quality conversations for your sales team—without increasing spend."
3. Align with Their Priority
PPS requires you to tie your solution to what is most urgent for the buyer right now.
Is it:

- **Speed to market?**
- **Saving budget?**
- **Hitting investor milestones?**
- **Hiring and scaling teams?**

? Example: Perfozi SDR Hiring Pitch to an Ahmedabad IT Firm

Priority Insight:
"We need ramp-up fast—we're shortlisting investors."
Pitch Delivered:
"Our trained SDRs can start delivering qualified meetings within 15 days—with weekly reporting to show traction fast."

Result: Deal closed in one follow-up.

4. Prepare Proof Specific to Their Persona

Don't drown them in random case studies.

Pick proof points that mirror their situation as closely as possible.

Options:

- **Similar industry**
- **Similar company size**
- **Similar challenges**

Use:

- **Short customer success stories**
- **Snippets of data**
- **Testimonials from peers they'll recognize**

? Example: Digital Sales Room for a Fintech Prospect

Included:

- **1 Fintech-specific landing page**
- **2 fintech client success snapshots**
- **1 fintech founder testimonial video**

Result: Immediate positive feedback and second meeting booked.

? Precision Persona Strategy (PPS) Cheatsheet

Step	What to Ask Yourself Before the Pitch
Profile	Who am I speaking to—not just title, but mindset?
Pain	What pain are they *already feeling* every day?
Priority	What's keeping them up at night *right now*?
Proof	Which client story feels like their mirror?

Precision Persona Strategy (PPS) Cheatsheet

? Advanced PPS Tactics

? Use persona-specific opening lines:
Start with a fear, frustration, or ambition relevant to their role.

? Create mini-pitch variants:
One version for Founders, another for CMOs, another for HR Heads.

? Update personas quarterly:
Buyer priorities shift fast. PPS is a living system, not a set-and-forget tool.

? Prepare Proof Libraries:
Organize case studies by industry, role, and pain point—so you can plug-and-play fast.

? Final Thought:

"The more precisely you pitch, the more effortlessly you close."
— Vikas Jain

Mastering Precision Persona Strategy (PPS) isn't about working harder. It's about working sharper—understanding that each pitch should feel custom-built for the person hearing it.

And when you use PPS properly, every meeting feels less like a **"presentation"**...

And more like a prescription—for exactly what they already know they need.

The Missing Ingredient—why Empathy Wins In Sales

"People will forget what you said, forget what you did, but never forget how you made them feel."
— Maya Angelou

In all my years building pitches, closing deals, and coaching sales teams at Marastu, Comfroi, and Perfozi, one truth has become crystal clear:

The ultimate sales advantage isn't a better product, a flashier presentation, or even a lower price.

It's empathy.

If you want to consistently pitch better, close faster, and build loyal clients who stay and refer—you must learn not just to think like a salesperson but to feel like a buyer.

And that shift changes everything.

? What Is Empathy in Sales?

Empathy is the ability to genuinely understand and share the feelings, concerns, and motivations of your buyer.

It means:

- **Seeing the world through their eyes**
- **Understanding their fears**
- **Appreciating their hopes**
- **Feeling their pressure—not just hearing it**

Empathy isn't "being nice" to close the deal.
It's about connecting deeply so that your pitch becomes a solution they trust, not a product you push.

? The Science Behind Empathy in Sales

Psychological Insight:

Studies show that empathy triggers the release of oxytocin in the brain—the trust hormone.

- **Buyers are biologically wired to trust people who:**

- **Listen carefully**
- **Mirror their emotions**
- **Validate their concerns**

When you lead with empathy, you lower resistance, increase emotional safety, and open pathways to collaboration.

? Why Empathy Is Your Ultimate Sales Weapon

Reason	Impact on Sales
Builds faster trust	Buyers feel heard and respected
Uncovers deeper pains	Buyers reveal real issues they hide from most sellers
Positions you as a partner, not a vendor	Elevates you above competition
Creates loyalty beyond contracts	Clients stay longer and refer more

Why Empathy Is Your Ultimate Sales Weapon

? How to Practice Real Empathy in Your Sales Process

1. Ask Questions You Genuinely Care About
Not scripted questions.
Real, thoughtful ones.
Instead of:
"What's your current process?"
Try:
"What part of your current process is frustrating or holding you back most?"
2. Listen Beyond the Words
Often what the buyer says isn't the full story.
Listen for:

- **Tone of voice**
- **Hesitations**

· **Emotional weight behind words**

Empathic listening means hearing not just the facts—but the feelings.

3. Validate Their Emotions (Not Just Their Problems)

Instead of rushing to "solve" as soon as they share a pain, first validate.

Say:

"That sounds incredibly frustrating. You're not alone—many leaders I work with feel the same pressure."

Validation creates emotional safety.

Only after that, offer your solution.

4. Mirror Their Priorities

Use their words.

Frame your pitch in their language, not yours.

If they say, "Our biggest worry is scaling without burning out," then later in your pitch, say:

"Let's talk about how we can help you scale without risking burnout across your team."

Mirroring makes buyers feel seen and supported.

? Real-World Examples of Empathy Winning Deals

? Marastu Video Call with a New York Fintech Client

Prospect was under extreme pressure from investors.

Instead of diving into service offerings, I said:

"Sounds like you're carrying a lot right now, especially with quarterly targets.

Would it help if we framed our solution purely around helping you hit those specific KPIs first—and expanded later?"

? Result:

Immediate emotional release on their side.

We secured a 3-month pilot project that expanded into a 12-month contract.

? Perfozi Discovery Call with an Ahmedabad-Based Startup

The founder mentioned struggling with "trust issues" from previous bad hires.

Instead of saying, "Our candidates are better," I said:

"I completely understand that. After all, one bad hire isn't just about money lost—it's trust broken.
That's why with Perfozi, we coach every SDR weekly alongside you, so you're never left wondering where things stand."

? Result:

Founder said:

"You get what I'm worried about more than any other recruiter we've spoken to."

They signed a retainer immediately.

? Empathy Phrases You Can Use Naturally

Phrase	When to Use
"That sounds tough—I appreciate you sharing that."	When hearing pain points
"It makes complete sense you're feeling that way."	When encountering fear/resistance
"If I were in your role, I'd probably be thinking the same thing."	To show alignment
"Let's create a plan that feels safe and aligned to your goals."	When proposing next steps

Empathy Phrases You Can Use Naturally

? The Empathy Advantage in Precision Persona Strategy (PPS)

Remember your Precision Persona Strategy?
Empathy takes it from mechanical to magical.

When you:

- **Profile the persona**
- **Understand their pain**
- **Prioritize their urgency**
- **Provide proof**

AND you do it all through the lens of genuine care—
Your pitch becomes irresistible.

Because you're not just offering value.
You're offering understanding.

? Final Thought:

"Empathy in sales is not a soft skill.
It's the sharpest tool you have."
— Vikas Jain

When you approach your prospects with empathy—not tricks, not pressure—you won't just close more deals.

- **You'll build deeper relationships.**
- **You'll create real partnerships.**
- **You'll become the kind of salesperson buyers love to say "yes" to.**

Empathy isn't the opposite of ambition.
It's the pathway to sustainable, unstoppable success.

Vikas Jain

Enter Caption